JACKED

TURBO

ARGED

JACKED

FORD FOCUS ST

Eric Stevens

MINNEAPOLIS

Darby Creek
A division of Lerner Publishing Group, Inc.
241 First Avenue North
Minneapolis, MN 55401 U.S.A.

Website address: www.lernerbooks.com

The images in this book are used with the permisison of:
Cover and interior photograph © Adrian Brannan/Fast Ford Magazine/Future/Getty Images.

Main body text set in Janson Text LT Std 12/17.
Typeface provided by Linotype AG.

Library of Congress Cataloging-in-Publication Data

Stevens, Eric, 1974–
Jacked : Ford Focus ST / by Eric Stevens.
pages cm. — (Turbocharged)
ISBN 978-1-4677-1246-0 (lib. bdg. : alk. paper)
ISBN 978-1-4677-1668-0 (eBook)
[1. Automobile racing—Fiction. 2. Muscle cars—Fiction.] I. Title.
PZ7.S84443Jac 2013
[Fic]—dc23 2013000972

Manufactured in the United States of America
1 – BP – 7/15/13

CHAPTER ONE

I ripped my jeans. My mom's going to kill me. Then she's going to ask me how I ripped my jeans, and I'll have to make something up. I can't tell her my jeans got caught on the windowsill.

When I was climbing out the window.

After midnight.

To drive across the city for a street race.

I'm at a red light, and I can already hear the revving engines and excited shouting of the spectators from a few blocks away.

"Come on, come on," I say to myself,

staring at the light, drumming on the steering wheel. It's my first time sneaking out of my house in the middle of the night—or any time of night, really.

It's the first time I've ever gone downtown on my own. I've taken the light rail twice with a couple of friends to see a baseball game. But all by myself, and long after nightfall? Never.

I'm not actually a bad kid. The thing is, I turned sixteen a couple of months ago. I've been saving my money for a long time because I knew that when I turned sixteen, I'd want a car.

I'd want a good car. I wouldn't be happy with some hunk of junk from 1983 that ran on diesel and went from zero to sixty in an hour and a half.

So as soon as I was allowed, I got a job and started saving money. With a little help from my grandparents, I had enough cash for a slightly used and pristine-condition Ford Focus ST. A turbocharged 250-horsepower 2-liter engine. Zero to sixty miles an hour in a hair over six seconds. The hottest hatchback on the U.S. market.

And that was before I hit the parts store: flash tuner, cold air intake, new cat back exhaust. I'll have the horsepower up to 300 before I'm through.

So why am I breaking out of my own house after midnight and tearing my jeans on the climb down the drainpipe? Because in the heart of the downtown financial district, where no normal person would dare to walk after closing time, all the hardcore tuners in this city are gathering.

Gathering to race.

"And if this light doesn't turn green," I say to myself, "I swear, I'm just going to go anyway."

I'm about to run—might as well, it's not like there's anyone around—when I hear footsteps running fast down the sidewalk. She's coming up from my left, from the direction of the financial district. She's older than me, but not by much—probably only a year or two out of high school. Her hair is jet black but streaked with red, and it's so long that it flies behind her and bounces all over as she runs.

And she's head to toe in bright orange leather. This girl is a car girl, no doubt. And she's heading right for me.

The light's green, but I can't find the gas pedal. I'm not sure I want to. Next thing I know, she slides across the hood.

"Hey!" I shout, because she might leave a dent. But she lands on the passenger side, no harm done, and pulls open the door.

"Drive," she snaps as she tosses her bag into the backseat. She slams the door and turns on me, her face twisted with fear and anger. She shoots a panicked glance over my shoulder at a man—too dark to see him clearly—running toward us a couple of blocks away. "Drive!"

"Wha—" I start. She cuts me off, balling her hand into a fist: "Just floor it!"

So what can I do? This girl is freaking out—not to mention insanely hot and into cars. Even though the light's turned red again, I slam the gas and, tires screeching, I take off.

CHAPTER TWO

I turn the wheel hard to the right—away from the guy running after this girl—and the little Ford squeals as we blast away from downtown.

"So," I say after a few moments of silence. "Who wa—"

"Just drive," she says. Then she coughs. "Please."

"Sorry," I say. She unbuckles her seatbelt.

"What are you doing?!" I shout, struggling to keep my eyes on the road.

"Relax," she says, but I can't, because she's turned around in her seat. She shoves her head past my shoulder, knocking my shifting arm as she does.

"Stop!" I say, but she just smiles—I catch it out of the corner of my eye as we bang onto the highway, back toward my suburban home.

For an instant, her leather-clad body is inches from my face, and then she's in the back seat, opening her gym bag.

I check her out in the rearview mirror. "That was pretty dangerous," I say.

"It just takes a little practice," she says, "and I do this once or twice a weekend. Chill." Then she unzips the front of her racing leathers.

"Whoa!" I say.

"Eyes on the road!" she snaps back, quickly reclosing her top. Then she gets a look out the front window. "Where are you going?"

"Um, my house?" I say.

"Uh-uh," she says. I'm struggling to keep my eyes on the road here, but they keep going back to the rearview, all on their own. "Take the exit for the north side. You can drop me off."

"Sure. Whatever you say."

There's a lot of moving around going on back there—the sounds of clothes slipping off and on, zippers going down and up. I click on the radio and turn it up. I even try driving with one hand, using the other to block my vision just enough so I can't glimpse the mirror.

"All right," she says over the blasting hip-hop. "I'm done." She leans forward and I quickly risk a glance. Now she's got on a black polo shirt and jeans—she still looks good, though not quite as race-car hot as she did. "Exit here."

I slip into the right lane—the highway is totally empty—and take the exit a little too fast. As I roll up to the light at the top of the ramp, she strains to check over her shoulder.

"Are we being followed or something?" I say.

"Huh?" she says, her eyes still on the exit ramp behind us.

"You keep looking behind us," I say. "Which way?"

"Oh," she says, with a little phony laugh in her voice. "It's nothing. Take a left, and then a quick right onto Third."

The light turns green, so I lift off the clutch and squeal through the big left turn. I pop it into second just as I hit Third, and the tires screech a little.

"So who was that guy?" I ask.

"Who?" she says. Again she looks behind us.

"The guy running after you," I say. "You going to tell me when to turn?"

"Pull over here," she says. I slam the brake and the clutch and shriek to a stop in front of an all-night diner. "Look," she says as she pops open the back door. "Don't worry about me, all right? And definitely don't worry about him."

She closes the door and starts for the diner's entrance, her gym bag hanging from her shoulder. I quickly lower the passenger window.

"Wait a minute," I call after her. She actually stops and turns around. "Are you in some kind of trouble or something? Was he your boyfriend or what?"

She sighs and rolls her eyes, but she walks back to my car and leans in through the window. "Look, I just didn't wanna deal tonight," she says. She talks through a smart little smile, like she's been around the block a hundred more times than I have, and she probably has. "I'm sorry I made you miss the race."

I shrug. "It's fine," I say. "So was he your boyfriend?"

She laughs. "He wishes."

I smile at her and say, "I'm James."

She leans in a little more. "Listen, James," she says. "When my shift ends, I will be without a ride. Wanna pick me up in about eight hours?"

My eyebrows pop up. "Sure." *School? What school?*

She winks and backs away from the car, then goes inside the diner.

She never even told me her name.

CHAPTER THREE

"Jamie!" Mom calls through my closed bedroom door. She's been calling me Jamie instead of James since the day I was born. For as long as I could talk, I've been telling her to call me James, but she won't change. That's moms, I guess.

I don't bother answering. It's just my typical school-day wake-up call. I'm not clear on why Mom distrusts my alarm clock, but a moment later it buzzes. I slap it, trusting my instincts to find the off button. It works on the third slap, and I sit up and scratch my head.

Last night comes rushing back at me. The sneaking out, the girl in orange leathers, the wee-hours drop-off on the north side of the city. I remember I'm not hurrying off to school today. I'm hurrying off to an all-night diner in a bad part of town.

By the time I get downstairs, Mom is halfway out the door. "You'll have to make your own breakfast," she says. She's in her best suit, with her laptop bag hanging from her forearm and her purse from her shoulder. "I have an early meeting." She makes a kissy sound at me and the next thing I hear is the rattling of her keys as she locks the door behind her.

I smile and grab the orange juice from the fridge. "No parental pressure this morning," I say to myself after a long drink from the bottle. I nearly drop it as I put it back.

Dad clears his throat.

"Dad!" I say, closing the refrigerator door. "What are you doing here?"

"I have the late shift tonight," he says. "Got anything special planned for your low-pressure morning?"

"Heh," I say, turning away to hide my red face. "Just heading to school, of course." I pretend to check my watch and whistle. "Better hurry, huh?" I say. I grab my book bag from next to the back door like I'm going to run out.

"Just a second, James," he says. Dad's always better about not calling me Jamie. "Let's talk about the jeans I just picked up off your floor."

"Did I forget to put them in the hamper?" I say, trying to laugh it off, but it's obvious: I'm busted.

"They're torn," he says. "A huge gash in the leg. Don't tell me this is the new thing in fashion."

"Ha," I say with a half shrug. "I guess they got caught on a nail."

"A nail?" Dad says, stepping right up to me and holding the jeans up between us. "Was the nail under the hood of your new car?"

"Huh?" I say, and he sniffs the jeans.

"Take a whiff of that," he says, holding

them up to my face, so I do. What choice do I have?

"What am I supposed to be smelling?" I say, but I know. They smell like exhaust and gasoline and motor oil—racing stuff.

"They reek," he says. "And before you think it's a good idea to keep up this act, I've already been outside. I found the torn shreds of your jeans on the downspout."

"Oh," I say, and lean against the wall next to the back door.

Dad lowers the jeans and turns around as he sighs. "Street racing is illegal."

"I didn't go to a race!" I protest, because I didn't. But I stop short before telling him about the mystery girl.

"Then where'd you go?" he asks, folding the jeans and leaving them on the counter. I guess Mom will patch them up. Great. Patched jeans. I'll look like a hobo.

I open my mouth to answer, but nothing comes out. Dad faces me and crosses his arms, a smirk on his face.

"The race," I finally say.

"Thought so," Dad says, nodding slowly. "Listen, you think I didn't go in for that stuff when I was a new driver? Of course I did. How do you think I know that smell so well? I also know how well it sticks to your clothes."

Ah, I think. *That girl brought the stench into my car*. She'd probably been tuning up or racing all night already.

"Believe me," Dad says. "I got busted once or twice when I was your age."

"Sorry," I say. "It won't happen again."

"See that it doesn't," Dad says. He puts a hand on my shoulder. It's meant to be firm and reassuring, but instead it just hurts a little. "You know, nowadays they take your license if you're busted racing."

"They do?" I say, half glad I never made it to the race. The truth is, I didn't intend to drive—just to watch and check out other guys' cars. But I doubt the police would care.

Dad nods. "We'll keep this from Mom," he says, "this time. Next time, you're on your own."

"There won't be a next time," I say. "I

promise. Now I really have to go," I add, checking the clock over his shoulder. It's nearly eight already.

"All right," he says, "have a good day at school. Stay out of trouble."

"I will," I say, fumbling with the door, my keys, and my bag. But I won't, because I'm not going to school. I'm going to a weird little diner in the bad part of town.

CHAPTER FOUR

I pull up to the curb at 8:30 on the dot, but I'm not actually sure what time exactly I dropped the mystery girl off. Am I early? Right on time?

Late?

I turn off the ignition and lean back with my arm out the window, my eyes on the diner's door.

"Do I go in?" I ask myself, trying to get a look inside. The glare on the windows is pretty strong, but I think I can just make out a figure in a black top hurrying between tables.

"I better not," I say. "She's working." I pull

my eyes off the diner and check out the street where I'm parked. A suped-up ride sits a few cars down on the other side of the street, in front of a little house with a beauty salon on the ground floor. Bright orange, with black detail, racing rims, ceramic brakes.

I check the time, glance at the diner once more, and climb out of my car to get a closer look. I can see this is no off-the-shelf kit job. It's a racing customized RX-8, with deep black tints, black rims, performance tires. I'm walking around to the passenger side, thinking I'll try to get a look at the inside through the tinted glass, when the driver's window hums and slides down.

"You need something, kid?" says the man at the wheel. He's rough looking—sunglasses, a scar across the bridge of his nose, and a shaved head. He's got on a black tank top, so I can tell right away that he's built. Probably got as much horsepower as his car.

"Sorry," I say, stepping back onto the sidewalk. "Didn't mean to creep around. I was just checking out your car. Turbocharged?"

"Yeah," he says, smiling and pulling off the sunglasses. "You know cars?"

"A little," I say. "Isn't that rough on the engine?"

He shrugs and smirks like it's no big thing. "For 400 horsepower, she'll make the necessary sacrifice. Power is everything."

He grunts a little as he reaches for the dash and pops the hood. Then he climbs out, opens the hood, and gives me the rundown.

"There's your turbo," he says. He points out the intake and the performance spark plugs. "Tuning chip brings those horses north of 400." He drops the hood and rests against the car, folding his arms across his chest. On his shoulder, there's a tattoo of a girl in an orange racing suit.

Huh.

"What about you?" he says. "You old enough to drive?"

"Yeah," I say with a little chuckle. I nod up the block.

"The ST?" he says, and he makes this impressed little grimace. I can tell he's just humoring me. "All stock?"

"I've made some upgrades," I say. "Wanna see?"

He glances at his watch—it's a nice one—and says, "Sure. I got a few minutes to kill." I lead him across the street, and as we walk he says, "I gotta ask you. You're a suburban kid—no offense. What are you doing hanging around here checking out cars on a school day?"

I laugh and explain. "Weirdest thing," I say. "I'm here to pick up a girl."

"Oh yeah?" he says, smiling like a weird uncle.

"I met her last night," I say. "Actually, I was heading to the race downtown—the drag race. You know it?"

He stops walking and grabs my arm—hard.

"Hey, what's—" I start to say. He cuts me off.

"A girl," he says. "Last night?"

I nod.

"She work here?" he says, glancing at the diner.

"I guess so," I say, and I pull my arm away.

He smiles—gentle—and puts up his hands like it's all good. "Look," he says. "You're a decent kid. You like cars, and that's good, and your little Focus probably can really move."

I shuffle a little. We're still in the street, and though no cars are coming, it puts me on edge.

"Here's an idea for you," he says, taking a step toward me and speaking real quietly. "Why don't you get into your little hatchback and see how fast it can move?"

"What?" I say.

"Yeah," he says. "Steer your car back to your junior high school and forget you ever met me or your mystery girl, all right?"

"I—"

Behind me, the diner doors fly open with a bang. "What is this?" she says—the mystery girl herself. I crane my neck and get a look at her. Her face is panicked and she's running toward us now.

"James, get away from him!" she shrieks, but it's too late. A huge arm wraps around my throat.

CHAPTER FIVE

"Let him go, Kells," the girl says, stopping short on the sidewalk. I'm down on the pavement now. The man's knee is pushing into the small of my back, and his arm is pulling at my throat. I can hardly believe what just happened, let alone scream for help.

"You coming with me?" he says. His voice is gruff and strained. "You gonna get in my car or you still planning to drive off with this little boy?"

"Yes," she says, hurrying over to us. "Yes, I'll come with you. Just let him go."

And just like that, he's off of me. I roll onto my back and see him standing over me, his arms crossed and a smug smile on his face. He must be pretty proud of himself, pinning a kid half his weight to the street.

The girl crouches and helps me stand up. She says quietly, "I'm sorry I got you into this, James. Just forget about me. Forget about all of this. Drive out of here and don't look back."

"Oh no," the guy says. I look over my shoulder at him, and he's climbing into his car. The door is still open as he turns the key and revs the engine. "He's coming with us."

"In that?" I say. I'm still rubbing my neck. "There's no room for me if she's coming with you."

He grins and leans down, pulling the trunk release. "She'll help you climb in."

"What?" I say, staring at the trunk lid as it rises.

"Come on," the girl says. "You can't be serious."

"I'm not the type to kid," he says. "Besides, I need a guarantee that you'll cooperate, gorgeous."

"I guarantee it," she says. "All right?"

"No," he grunts. With any trace of a smile gone, he tells me to get in.

It's a tiny trunk, but what can I do? I curl up best I can. My head is pressed up against a compact jack, and something big and hard is digging into my side.

The guy stands over me a minute, with one hand on the trunk lid. "I'll try not to hit the bumps too hard," he says, and then it's darkness.

* * *

I think he was lying. This little sports car, with its tight suspension and low ride, seems to hit every bump on the road to . . . wherever we're going. He takes every curve like this is the Monaco Grand Prix, and my head knocks into the metal jack over and over.

After what feels like an eternity, we come to a sudden stop. I expect the trunk to pop any second, but it doesn't. Instead I hear voices coming from the front seat. It's impossible to make out any words clearly, but I can tell when Kells is shouting—and he's shouting a lot.

A few minutes of shouting—from both of them—and then silence. He says a few things quietly, and she laughs. Then the driver's side door finally pops open. A moment later, so does the trunk lid.

"Out," he says. He doesn't even look at me. He just steps back, one hand on the trunk, ready to close it again. For a second, I wonder if he'll close it a little early, maybe take off my hand. But I climb out and brush myself off before he slams the lid down.

I see through the rear window that the girl is still in the car.

"Wait a minute," I say. I grab the guy's wrist before he can get back into the car. He snarls like an attack dog, and I quickly let go. "What's going on?"

She leans forward in her seat and catches my eye. "Don't worry about me," she says. "I'm fine."

"You sure?" I ask.

Suddenly the musclehead turns on me and grabs my shirt collar. He pulls my face close to his and slaps the back of his hand across my face. It stings, and I can feel a little cut on my cheek from his ring.

"Walk home," he growls. "Don't turn around. Erase me, her, and the last twelve hours of your pathetic life from your mind." He tosses me by the collar to the ground, opens the car door, and climbs in. The engine roars to life, the tires squeal, and burnt rubber fills my nostrils as he peels off down the road.

CHAPTER SIX

"Forget him?" I mutter to myself. I'm headed down the winding roads of the bluff toward the nearest city bus stop. "Forget *her*?"

That's never going to happen. Instead of forgetting them or the last twelve hours, I go over it all in my head.

Carjacked—sort of—by a gorgeous girl in the middle of the night.

A warning from Dad.

Cutting a morning of school to pick up the girl at work.

And, finally, being held hostage by a

muscular motorhead.

Now I'm standing at a bus stop clear across the city waiting for a public bus to bring me to school, bruises covering half my body.

Forget it? I don't think so.

"Where you been all morning?" says Liam when I drop my tray of hot lunch on the table. The bus ride was long and boring, and I was lucky to make it to school in time for taco lunch.

"You wouldn't believe me if I told you," I say. When I open my mouth to take a bite of my taco, the cut on my cheek opens again.

"You're bleeding," Liam says.

I pat it with a napkin. "It's not too bad," I say. "Some dude slapped me."

"Some dude?" Liam says. "Who? Someone in school?"

What can I do? I start with the night before—sneaking out to check out the race—and tell him everything that happened since.

"That's pretty unbelievable," Liam says.

"See?" I say.

"But I believe you," he goes on, "because I know who that guy is."

"How could you possibly?" I ask.

Liam leans back in his chair like he's a big shot. "Sean used to race," he says. Sean's his big brother. He moved to the coast two years ago to open a surf shop. I think he's working for a lawn care company now, so I guess it didn't work out.

"So?" I say.

"So that guy," Liam says, leaning forward like it's a big secret, "was probably Kelly Briggs."

"Yes!" I say, practically jumping out of my little plastic chair. "She called him Kells."

"Told you I knew," Liam says. "He's been around the scene for years."

"What's his story?" I ask. "Why's he such a jerk?"

"He's bad news," Liam says. "He's a parts dealer."

"What so bad news about that?"

"Stolen parts," Liam says. "At least, that's what Sean always said."

"Did Sean buy from him?" I ask.

"He never told me," he says. "But I'll tell you this: When Sean took off, we got a few phone calls at the house. Weird phone calls."

"What do you mean?" I ask.

"Blocked caller ID," Liam says. "Creepy voice on the other end, always asking for Sean and never leaving a number. The calls eventually stopped. I don't know if they found him or what."

"So you think it was Kells?" I ask. "You think Sean owed him money?"

Liam clears his throat. "All I know is, right before Sean left, he came home really late one night with a box of parts. The next day, he spent hours under the hood. And the next weekend, he was sure he'd win the midnight drag race."

"Did he?" I ask.

"Nope," Liam says. "Which means he didn't win any money."

"You think he was counting on winning to

pay Kells for the parts?" I say.

Liam shrugs. "Who knows."

I think this all over. If Sean couldn't pay back a guy like Kells, maybe that's why he took off for the coast so suddenly. I sure don't blame him for running from the guy.

"So what about the girl?" I whisper. "To be honest, I'm more interested in who *she* is."

"I have a guess," Liam says. He pushes the droppings from his tacos into a pile in the middle of his plate, then scoops it up. "I heard about a girl a couple years ago—Kim something. She had a bad accident during a race. Totally destroyed her car and Kells's. He blamed her, and he's been making her pay him back ever since."

"Wow," I say.

Liam cleans his plate and leans back, his hands folded behind his head. "It's probably not the same girl," he says. "But if she's mixed up with Kells, I'll tell you this: Stay away from her."

"But she saved me from him," I say. "She could have walked away when he had me pinned down in the street and she didn't. Besides, I think she's in some kind of trouble. I have to do something."

"Do what you gotta do," Liam says as he stands up to return his tray.

I check the clock: It's not even noon. It'll be a long day till school's out.

CHAPTER SEVEN

A little before four o'clock that afternoon, I pull up to the diner—the one on the north side of the city. I sit there in the driver's seat with the car running, just staring at the front of the place. I'm wondering if she's in there, if she'd be happy to see me, or if she'd pretend she didn't know me and tell me to bug off.

With a sigh, I turn off the car and climb out. The afternoon sun is bright, and when I pull open the diner door, the dimness inside makes me feel nearly blind. I stumble up to the host's stand.

"Eating alone?" says a woman's voice. It's not the girl from last night.

"I'm—" I start. Then I realize: I don't even know her name. My eyes begin to adjust to the low light, and I look around. It's a small diner, and I can see everyone inside. She's not here.

"Hello?" says the host. She's an older woman, with her hair up in a bun. She's wearing a black shirt just like the one my mystery girl put on in the backseat of my car last night.

"Sorry," I say. "I'm looking for someone who works here."

She leans forward as if to say, go on.

"I don't know her name," I say.

"Ah," she says. "Have you got a little crush on one of the waitresses?"

"What?" I say. "No, it's nothing like that. I know her. I just don't know her name."

"Sorry," she says, shuffling around some menus on the counter in front of her. "Can't help you."

"Fine," I say. "I'll just take a stool at the counter." Without waiting for a reply, I grab a seat and order a glass of pop.

"That's it?" says the waiter. He's not much older than me, and if he works with the mystery girl, he'd have to know her. He'd want to, anyway.

"Yeah, that's it," I say. Before he can walk off, I add, "Hey, I'm looking for a girl who works here."

"Are you?" he says without looking at me, his tone flat and bored.

"Yeah," I say. "She's got dark hair with red streaks and she's really into cars."

At the word *cars* he looks up.

"You know who I mean?" I say.

He quickly brings back his bored look. "No idea," he says, but I can tell he's lying. "No one like that works here."

He walks off to get my drink. Less than a minute later, a glass of cold pop is in front of me. He drops a straw next to it and says, "Enjoy," as bored as ever.

I sigh and tap the straw on the counter to get the paper off. At the same time, a busboy—my age or younger—comes up next to me to clear an empty plate and coffee cup from the place beside me.

He glances around and then says real quietly, "Hey, I know who you're looking for."

I nearly spit out my pop. "Who is she?" I say.

"Not so loud," he says. "Pay your check and I'll talk to you outside. I get off in two minutes."

Then he disappears into the kitchen. I down my pop so fast it burns my throat and drop a pair of dollar bills on the counter. Then I head outside to my car.

The busboy comes from around back and waves me over.

A weird guy at a diner asks me to talk to him in an alley, and I follow. What else can I do?

"If anyone saw me talking to you, they'd kill me," he says.

"Why?" I ask. "What's the big deal with this girl?"

"It's not the girl," he says. "Everyone saw what happened yesterday. It's all anyone in the diner's talking about."

"It is?"

He nods. "Listen, you don't want to get involved in this."

"I already I am," I point out. I keep having to point that out. "Please. If you can tell me how to find her, tell me."

"She doesn't work here anymore," the busboy says. "After that scene in the street yesterday, the owner fired her."

"Wow," I say. "That's not exactly fair."

"Look, he wasn't happy about it," the busboy insists, "but he can't exactly have Kells showing up here all the time and making trouble."

"Then you know Kells," I say in a quiet voice.

He nods again and leans in close. "I don't know where the girl is. But if you want to find Kells, I can tell you how."

"Find Kells?" I say. "You mean the guy who pinned me to the street and tossed me in his trunk? Why would I want to find him?"

The busboy snickers and takes a slip of

paper from the pocket of his jeans. "If you change your mind, here."

I glance at the paper as he puts it in my hand. "What is this?"

"A phone number," he says, "and a pass code. Text it. He'll call."

With that, he turns away and slips in through the diner's side door, leaving me standing in the alley with a secret phone number. A number that would probably have the police dragging me in for questioning.

CHAPTER EIGHT

That night after supper with Mom—Dad has the late shift again—I sit on my bed, staring at my phone in my hand. In my other hand, I'm holding that slip of paper the busboy gave me.

I take a deep breath and think about the girl: I can still picture her sliding across the hood of my Focus. I can picture her climbing into the backseat to change. I can picture her slamming through the doors of the diner to try to save me from Kells.

What am I waiting for? I think. *Of course I have to try to reach Kells, if that's the only way I can make sure she's okay.*

I put the number down next to me and send the text. Then I continue staring at the phone, waiting for it to ring.

And waiting.

I check the clock—thirty minutes have passed. I wait some more. I even crack a textbook and try to do my math homework. But it's hopeless, because I keep checking my phone.

When ten o'clock rolls around, my phone's still silent aside from a couple of messages from Liam. Mom and Dad stick their heads in to say good night.

"Don't stay up too late," Mom says. She blows me a kiss and retreats.

"How was work?" I ask Dad.

He shrugs. "Get your homework done?" he asks. I nod.

"Get some sleep," he says, and he pulls his head out and closes the door.

My shoulders sag as I check my phone one more time. Nothing. I sigh and get ready for bed.

* * *

Thirty minutes later, my teeth are brushed and I'm under the covers. I switch off the light and stare into the darkness. I'm exhausted—it's been a weird couple of days. But just as I drift off, my phone starts shimmying on the table next to the bed.

I grab it, nearly knocking my lamp to the floor in the process.

"Hello?" I say.

"Who's this?" says a gruff voice I don't recognize.

Is this Kells? I can't even tell.

"Um," I say, my voice cracking, "I got your number from a friend. I'm looking for Kells."

The voice doesn't respond, but it sounds like someone's covering the phone and talking to someone else.

After a couple of minutes, I say, "Hello?"

The gruff voice comes back. "All right," he says. "Come to the race tonight. Be early."

"Tonight?" I say. It's almost eleven.

"Did I stutter?" says the voice. There's a

short beep, and the phone call is over.

"Great," I mutter to myself, sitting up. "Looks like I'm sneaking out again."

CHAPTER NINE

It's harder tonight. As I slip out of my bedroom, I can see the flickering light from the TV under my parents' bedroom door. They're still awake. Hopefully the TV will drown out the sound of the creaking wooden steps as I head downstairs.

I really don't want to try going down the drainpipe again.

As I slip outside and see my Focus sitting at the top of the driveway, it hits me. Even if the TV managed to disguise my footsteps, it'll wake half the neighborhood when I crank that car up. But I have a plan. It's lucky I backed in to my parking spot this afternoon.

I quietly get into the car. I even leave the door open a little so I don't have to slam it. Then, without starting it up, I slip it into neutral. Once I drop the parking brake, the car rolls out of the driveway as quiet as a mouse.

I roll down our street for a good quarter of a mile. Then I push down on the clutch, put the car into second gear, and slam the gas as I release the clutch. An old-fashioned jump start. The car coughs and then roars to life, and I'm off.

* * *

I'm a couple of the blocks from the race start line downtown when I come to a red light. I know it's silly, but the tiniest part of me thinks my mystery girl might come running again. That she might slide across the hood and climb in. Of course, she doesn't. The light changes from red to green, and I drive on.

When I'm around the corner from the start line, I pull over where it's nice and dark and try to get a look at what's happening.

There are four cars there already, with their lights off and drivers and passengers out and standing around. One of the cars I recognize at once. It's Kells's Mazda. The man himself leans on the driver's door with his arms crossed, his head back, laughing loud and clear.

It's like he's daring someone to hear them gathered here, breaking at least two laws and getting ready to break a whole bunch more.

Kells's trunk is open—I get a chill just looking at it—and lots of small boxes are stacked up inside it and on the street behind the car. This must be the merchandise. One of the other guys is counting out some money.

So the number I texted must be for customers, I think. *They'll be expecting me to have cash, ready to buy something.*

I don't have much—a couple of bucks and a fifty dollar bill Dad makes me carry folded up in my wallet for an emergency. This is an emergency, I decide, and I start walking over. He must have something for under fifty, right?

But just as I step out of the shadows near my car, something goes down. One of Kells's customers says something or does something wrong. Maybe he doesn't have enough money, or maybe he insulted Kells. Who knows? All I know is, Kells grabs him by the collar, just like he grabbed me.

I stop short. One of the other guys—he must work for Kells—comes up behind the guy and holds his arms. Then Kells slams his fist into the poor guy's gut. He cries out and then folds over in pain. But Kells isn't done. He pulls his fist back again. This time he gets the guy in the chin.

"No!" I call out. I have no idea what kind of a moron I am, but by the time I've clamped my hand over my mouth, it's way too late. They've seen me.

Kells's henchman drops the poor guy with the busted jaw. Kells starts running toward me.

What can I do? I turn around, get into my car, crank it to life, and peel out of there. And suddenly I'm in my first car chase.

CHAPTER TEN

I'm lucky to have a head start. By the time Kells and his buddies get into their cars, I'm a couple of blocks away. Still, with that turbocharged RX-8, and probably a trunkful of nitrous, Kells will catch me pretty quick.

I take a turn onto 13th Street, going way too fast. My tires scream and the rear end sticks out as I slide around the corner. Somehow I survive, and I slam it into third gear as I roar up to forty miles an hour. Soon I'm screaming through the abandoned streets of the warehouse district, doing sixty in a thirty.

But what can I do? If they catch me . . . What they did to that other guy . . .

I check the rearview, and I was right: Kells is having no trouble keeping up. He's still ten blocks back, but he's gaining, and with no other cars around, he'll have no trouble finding me. The roar of my engine will be easy to hear.

The light up ahead is red, but I can't stop. He'll be on my tail in no time if I do that.

But suddenly I have no choice—someone is walking across the street. I slam on the brake and the clutch. The tail slips and slides, threatening to spin around and send me into a 360 or worse. I grip the wheel with all my strength, trying to keep the car stable and to stop before I reach the crosswalk.

Ahead, the girl crossing the street is waving frantically, screaming at me.

It's her. It's my mystery girl. I finally squeal to a stop inches from her. She runs to the passenger side and gets in.

Without waiting for hellos or for her

seatbelt to click, I slam the car into first, stomp on the gas, and shriek off around the corner, hoping to lose Kells.

"Fancy meeting you here," she shouts over the scream of my engine.

I force a smile but keep my eyes on the road.

"You'll never lose him like this," she says as we tear around another corner, onto Grand Boulevard.

"You got a better idea?" I say. I grab a hard U-turn around a divider. Now we're flying along the boulevard back toward Kells—but he's on the other side and going the wrong way.

"As a matter of fact," she says, grabbing the hand strap as we squeal back onto 13th Street, "I do."

"I'm all ears," I say, shifting into fourth and then fifth. Fifth gear on a downtown street—I should go to jail forever.

"Take a right, next light," she says. I obey. A half block later, she leans forward and points at a driveway: a narrow alley between office buildings. "In there."

What can I do? I hit the brake, shift into second, and crawl into the alley. It's a dead end. About ten yards in front of me are a Dumpster and a wall.

"Now what, genius?" I snap.

She smiles and leans across the gear shift. With a hand on my leg, she reaches over, switches off the lights, cuts the ignition, and puts a finger to her lips: Shhh. . . .

"Are you crazy?" I shout. But she shushes me again and cocks her head toward the back window.

I turn in my seat and she turns in hers. We watch as two cars—Kells's and another—speed by our alley. A couple of minutes later, they speed by again.

I wait a few minutes, silently. All I can hear is the roar of Kells's engine fading and the mystery girl's breathing. The smells of leather and gasoline and exhaust swell inside the car, along with hints of the garbage in the Dumpster and the girl's shampoo: citrus.

"Think he gave up?" I whisper.

"Probably," she says. "Let's wait a little more, just to be sure."

So we wait.

"It's a good thing you got the boring blue exterior instead of the bright orange," she says.

"Boring?" I say.

"This looks like a car my grandma would drive," she says. "No offense."

"Not offended at all," I say with a grin. "Though I don't think your grandma drives a machine with close to 300 horsepower and 300 pounds of torque. Besides, I'd rather look like a grandma than have Kells's fist in my teeth."

"Was he handing out beatings tonight?" she asks.

I nod. "What about you?" I ask. "Why were you walking around the warehouse district?"

"I live there," she says. "I was just walking home from the light rail station."

"I'll drop you off, then," I say. "It's probably safe. I don't hear Kells's engine anymore."

She leans back in her seat. "Yeah, he'll

want to be at the start line anyway," she says. "He's more interested in selling parts and placing bets than beating you up."

"That's all right with me," I say, about to start the car.

"Wait a sec," she says. "I never get to drive anymore. Always riding the train or the bus."

"And?"

"Let me have a turn," she says.

"Seriously?" I say, my finger frozen on the start button.

"What?" she says. "You don't think a girl can drive?"

So what can I do? I put up my hands, climb out of the car, and let her climb over. She starts it up. The instant I'm seated in the passenger seat, she throws the shifter into R, squeals out into the street, and flips us around.

"Nice move," I say.

"You ain't seen nothing yet," she says, grinning.

We're off, and this girl can drive.

She takes me to a paring ramp, way up to the big wide-open top story. She drifts, shows off with hand-brake turns and parks, and finally does a wicked hand-brake U-turn that nearly knocks my head off.

"Okay, okay," I say. "Before you shred my tires, let's call it a night."

But she's grinning ear to ear, and I can't help grinning with her. She's obviously having a blast.

"All right," she says. "Thanks for the good time. I'll head to my place, OK?"

⁂

It's a short drive, and she pulls up to the curb right near where I picked her up after nearly running her over. Her building is a three-story tenement. The place looks pretty run-down. But she's on her own, instead of living with her parents, so I'm pretty jealous.

We meet face-to-face in front of my car, her on her way to the building, me on the way to the driver's seat.

"Thanks again, James," she says.

The car's headlights are washing over us.

"Listen," I say. "I wanted to tell you. I didn't come out tonight to buy parts from Kells or see the race."

"No?" she says.

I shake my head. "I came hoping to find you," I say. "I wanted to make sure you were okay."

She shrugs one shoulder and smirks. "I'm all right," she says. "Looking for a new job, hardly making rent. But, you know. I'm all right."

"Good," I say.

She smiles at me, then slips past me toward the sidewalk, running her fingers down my arm as she passes.

"Wait," I call after her before she gets inside. I hurry to the bottom of her stoop. "Your name. I don't know your name."

"Kimberly," she says. "Kimberly Dutton."

"Kim," I say. "Then it is you. You're the girl who had the accident."

Her face falls and she looks at the ground.

"Sorry," I say. "That was a pretty stupid thing to say."

"It's fine," she says.

Then it hits me.

"Maybe I can help. I can race him. I'll bet the whole debt."

"You?" she says. "Not to be rude, James, but he'll destroy you."

"Thanks a lot," I say, feeling pretty dumb.

She steps down the stoop and takes my hand. "You're very sweet, but his car is suped up way beyond yours. And his skill behind the wheel . . ."

"All right, I get it," I say.

"Look, it's not a terrible idea," she says, "but I'll have to drive." My eyebrows go up and she sticks her tongue out. "I might win."

"Fair enough," I say.

"And we'll have some work to do between now and the race," she says. "That little Mazda of his has got more than meets the eye under the hood."

"I figured," I say.

"Gimme your phone," she says, so I do. She types in her name and number. Her phone rings in her pocket and she shuts it off. "We'll talk tomorrow and start work."

With that, she pats my hand and slips inside. The door closes behind her. It locks with a click, and I get back in the car. I drive home on cloud nine.

But despite how good I was feeling in the car, I'm feeling a whole lot worse when I pull up to the house.

Because the front porch light is on. And so is the light in the living room and in the kitchen. And the front door is open, and both my parents are standing in it, with their arms crossed and very angry looks on their faces.

I'm so busted. And so grounded.

CHAPTER ELEVEN

The next day is Saturday. The plan had been to head out and meet Kim to work on the car. But with the grounding, that's not going to happen. I text Kim to let her know before I head down for breakfast.

My parents glare at me over their coffee cups. I grab a glass of juice and decide to ride out the grounding in the basement, in front of the TV. I'm an hour into a marathon of British car shows when I hear the doorbell ring. Dad's footsteps clunk over my head. I pause the show and stick my head through the basement door.

"Hello," Dad says. I can't see who's at the front door. "Can I help you?"

"Um, I'm looking for James," says a girl's voice. My stomach flips as I practically fall up the rest of the steps and hurry to the door.

"Oh, hi," Kim says with a smile.

"What are you doing here?" I ask.

She shrugs. "I took the bus."

Dad looks at me and I flash a nervous smile. "Um, this is Kim," I tell him.

"I'm a friend from school," she says quickly. "We're working on a project together."

"Oh yeah?" Dad says. He looks at me and puts his fists on his hips. "What kind of project?"

"For auto shop," I say.

"I didn't think you ever had auto shop homework," he says. "The work is done at the school garage, isn't it?"

"Ha," I say. "Usually it is. But, um, Kim is going to help me install some parts in the Ford, and—"

"Ah," Dad says. "A little extra credit?"

"Exactly!" I say. "Extra credit."

Dad turns to Kim. "Just a second, okay? He'll be right out."

She smiles as the door closes in her face. Mom's straining to hear from her seat in the kitchen, so Dad takes me by the arm away from the door and into the living room.

"Girlfriend?" he asks.

"No," I say. "Totally not."

His eyebrows go up.

"Dad, I swear," I say. "She's just here to help me with the car. She knows cars."

He twists up his mouth and leans his head back. But I think he's coming around. "All right," he says.

"Yes," I whisper in triumph.

"But you stay in the driveway or the garage," he says. "No test drives. No quick spins. And if the two of you come inside, you stay on the ground floor where your mom and I can see you. Get me?"

"Yup," I say, hurrying for the door. I step into my sneakers and slip outside as I quickly add, "Thanks, Dad."

⁂

Kim's already got the hood popped and the car off the ground, on ramps.

She's crouched in the driveway beside a big cardboard box that looks like it's been through a couple of moves and maybe a flood or two.

"What's that?" I say, stepping up next to her.

"Some parts I salvaged from the wreck," she says. "I haven't gone through them in ages. Hurts my heart too much."

I squat beside her. She pulls out the gear shift and grins. "Here's what we need," she says. The shift knob is bright orange with tiger stripes. On the side is a little orange button of translucent plastic.

"Kind of garish, isn't it?" I say.

She gasps like she's offended, and I laugh.

"It's *beautiful*," she says, "and it matches my racing suit. It once matched my car, too."

"Your car had tiger stripes?" I say.

"It was orange," she says. "An orange Focus with black detail and interior."

"Wow," I say. I sit back. "No wonder you can drive mine so well."

She nods and digs around the parts box. "And everything in here will be compatible, too," she says.

I pick up the shift knob. "What's the button for?" I ask.

She smiles and stands up, walks around to the far side of my car, and comes back with another box. I immediately spot a big white tank: nitrous.

"Where did you get that?" I say in a loud whisper.

"I splurged," she says, "for you."

"Are you crazy?" I say as she puts the box down between us in the driveway. "How much was it?"

"It's on me," she says. "I emptied my tip jar, also known as my life savings, for this."

"Kim," I say, "you can't do this. You just told me you're—well, it's so much money."

"If we win this race against Kells," she says, "it'll be more than worth it."

I sigh. She's right, but I know a nitrous kit

could cost almost a thousand bucks.

"Don't look so nervous," she says, patting my knee. "We're talking about 75 hp here. It's what we have to do to win."

I nod. "Thanks," I say.

"Uh-uh," she says, standing up. "I did this for me, James, not for you. I have to win this race."

Good point, I think. Then we get to work.

* * *

Kim's there all day, and she knows what she's doing. We get the lines installed, put the new shifter in—tiger-stripe knob and nitrous button included—and add the tank in the trunk. Mom even brings us sandwiches for lunch. Before I know it, it's gotten dark.

"Do we go to the race tonight?" I ask. "Can you beat him in this?"

"I can," Kim says, "but we're not racing him like that."

"What do you mean?" I ask.

"This is going to be just us and him," she

says. "No stoplights. No spectators."

"Why not?" I ask.

"Because when I show up at the start line," she says, "things get ugly."

Ugly? I think. *Her? No way.*

She pulls out her phone, and I watch her send off a text to Kells. It's got a time, a place, and a long number.

"That's not the pass code I got," I say.

"That's not a code," she says as she hits send. "It's how much we'll bet."

"Whoa," I say, because that is a big bet.

"He'll know what it means," she says. A moment later, her phone beeps. She reads his reply. "We're on."

"That was quick," I say. "I think you get under his skin."

"You could say that," she says. "So—tonight at midnight. You'll have to give me a ride. The bus doesn't go out that way."

I take a deep breath. "All right. I'll pick you up."

Dad gives me special permission to drive Kim home. But when we're nearby her place, she tells me to pull over.

"What's wrong?" I ask, sliding up to the curb.

She nods toward her building. There's a coupe parked in front.

"That's one of Kells's boys," she says. "He's probably waiting for me."

"Why?" I say.

"Who knows," she says. "But I doubt it's to wish me luck in the race."

"Ah," I say. "We can wait till he leaves."

She shakes her head. "We'll be waiting all night. We'll have to go back to your place."

"What?" I say. "No way. My parents will not be okay with you staying over."

"All right," she says with one hand on the door handle. "I guess I'll just walk over there. He'll probably rough me up. Maybe break my shifting hand."

I sigh and she grins. "Fine," I say. "But you have to wait outside, till they go to bed. Okay?"

"You got it," she says, rebuckling her seatbelt.

CHAPTER TWELVE

So that's how I wound up hiding a gorgeous nineteen-year-old girl in my bedroom for two hours. Mom and Dad are in their room watching a sitcom, thinking Kim left an hour ago. Meanwhile, she's sitting at my desk, leaning on her elbow, watching me while I watch her.

"Let's watch some TV," she says.

I shake my head. "No way. It'll wake my parents."

She groans and drums her fingers on the desktop. She pulls a lock of her hair across her face and sniffs it. “I smell like a mechanic,” she says.

“You are a mechanic,” I say.

“Not professionally.”

“Should be,” I point out.

“Maybe,” she says, “but right now, all I want is a shower.”

“No way,” I say, but she’s already standing up and digging around in her bag. She pulls out her racing leathers.

“Why did you bring those?” I ask, standing up from the bed.

“Just in case,” she says. “Where’s the bathroom?”

“Kim,” I say. “My parents will wake up. And when someone’s in the shower and it’s not me, I think they’ll probably get suspicious.”

“I’ll tell you what,” she says as she opens the bedroom door and peeks into the hall. She’s halfway out of the room. “While I shower, you hide in your closet, just in case. They’ll assume it’s you if you’re not in your room.”

“Showering this late?” I say. “Why would I shower this late?”

"Because you smell like a mechanic, too," she points out. And while I'm sniffing my shirt, she slips out and closes the door. A minute later, I hear the water running.

"Great," I say. But what can I do? With a sigh, I step into the closet to wait for her to finish.

Kim takes long showers, it turns out, so I have a lot of time to sit on the closet floor with my knees pulled up. And while I'm there, I can think about nothing but her in the shower. I'm wondering if I'll ever shake that image—or if I'll ever want to—when my bedroom door creaks open.

"Don't come out yet," Kim whispers through the closet door. "I'm not dressed."

"Oh boy," I say, and I wait a little longer. Finally the closet door swings open. Kim's standing there above me, decked out in her orange leather racing suit. Her hair is still wet and she's pulling on her gloves.

"How do I look?" she says.

My jaw drops, and I guess that says it all. Besides, it's time to go.

CHAPTER THIRTEEN

It takes us about twenty minutes to reach the start line Kim chose. It's way out past the western suburbs in one of these uninhabited neighborhoods. There's a bunch around the city now. Developers built them and then no one bought the houses. So they just sit there, quiet and pristine.

They make good racetracks, too, with their hilly and curvy roads. For my hot hatch and Kells's Mazda, a course like this is the perfect test.

As we pull into the neighborhood, Kim

nods toward the busted-up sign that once showed the name of the development. It's been vandalized beyond legibility now. Kells is parked next to it. He and one of his thugs are leaning on the side of the Mazda.

I park, and Kells walks toward the car. He opens the door for Kim to climb out.

"I wasn't sure you'd make it," he says to her.

"Are we late?" I say, checking the time on the dashboard. It's still a couple of minutes before midnight.

"That's not what he means, James," Kim says, coming around the front of the car as I climb out. "He means he thought his thug would have broken my leg or something."

Kells chuckles. "That's ridiculous," he says. Then he turns to me. "Ready to race, little boy?"

I put my hands up. "You got the wrong driver, man," I say. I point at Kim. "She texted you, not me."

"Right," says Kim. She climbs into the driver's seat and buckles in. "You got a course mapped out?"

"You don't seem to understand," Kells says. "This is the boy's car, and the boy will do the driving."

"What?" Kim says. "You making up the rules as you go now?"

The thug with Kells laughs. "Standard street rules," he says. "Your title, your car, you're driving."

Kim gives me a long look and takes a deep breath. Then she says quietly, "Can you do this?"

My eyebrows go up. I look from her to Kells's snickering face. Then I nod. "I can do it." For her, I can do it.

Kim climbs out and I get back behind the wheel. Kells leans on my open window. "You know this area?" he asks, and I nod. "Good." Then he goes over the course quickly. I listen carefully, because chances are he's done this before, and I've never driven here at all.

"Let him go around one time," Kim says. "Let him find the curves and all that."

"No way," Kells says. "One race, one

winner. That's it."

He walks off and gets into his Mazda. Kim comes to the window. "Remember," she says. "It ends in a nice long straightaway. Push the button when you enter the straight, try to get there first."

"I'll do my best," I say.

She smiles. "I know you will," she says. Then she leans in and kisses my cheek. "Good luck."

I'm gonna need it.

Kells and I pull up to the start line. Kells has marked it with yellow spray paint. He lets Kim call the start.

Kim stands at the side of the road, holding up a bright orange tiger-striped handkerchief. She looks me in the eye, winks, and then drops her hand. The race is on.

CHAPTER FOURTEEN

Kells pulls away from the start and takes the first curve on the inside, cutting me off. I do my best to stay right on his bumper, but I'm a newbie—staying that close takes the kind of courage behind the wheel I don't have yet.

On the first short straight, he pulls away, but the next curve is a tight one—a full U-turn into the first uphill. The Mazda does all right, but my little hatch takes the curve like it's on rails and fires up at the hill. At the top, the road whips around again. Before long, I'm up alongside Kells.

I like the feel of Kim's shift knob in my hand, but my thumb keeps grazing that nitrous button. I'm itching to press it—to feel the extra 75 hp and to surge past Kells. But I have to wait. If I take that sudden burst of speed on a curve, I'll definitely end up on an overgrown lawn—or in an abandoned living room.

And that's not counting the damage I'd do to my engine if I use the nitrous under 4,000 RPMs.

Kells is right next to me as we come around a wide curve to the left. I'm on the inside. From up here on the hill, I can see all the way down to the finish. The last straight up to the finish line, where Kim and Kells's thug are waiting, is coming up quick.

Kells sees it, too. He risks a pass when he takes the inside on the next curve to the right. I slip away and take the curve wide to avoid a crash. Kells slides out in front of me, forcing me back to the right. That means on the last curve, I'll be on the outside.

I hope my handling beats his. I know I'll

have to hit the curve perfectly and bravely if I'm going to pass him for the straight.

We take the final curve neck and neck, and the instant we hit the straight, I downshift to second so my revs are up to 4K. Then I clench my teeth, say a quick prayer that Kim and I got the thing installed just right, and press that little orange button.

The surge kicks my head back as I pull away. Kells hits his nitrous, too, an instant later, but it's not enough. I see Kim up ahead, in her bright orange leather. She's jumping up and down, waving her arms in celebration.

I check the side-view mirror. Kells is a full car length behind me, and he's not gaining. I'm up into third, fourth, fifth gear. I release the nitrous as I find sixth, and Kim hurries onto the grass as I fly across the finish line.

I'm grinning like an idiot as I quickly downshift and brake, then turn and stop. Kells comes to a stop nearby. He pounds his fists on his steering wheel, fuming that he lost.

But Kim is still cheering, jumping up and down as she runs over to my car. As I climb out, she throws her arms around me and plants a kiss right on my mouth. I can hardly breathe—till a huge hand claps on my back, making me cough.

"Nice race," says Kells. He shoulders Kim aside and faces me.

"Thanks," I say, feeling pretty proud. "And Kim's debt?"

He glances at her sideways. "It's clear," he says, then adds through a sneer: "But she better not show up at the races for a while."

"Don't worry about that," Kim says. "Not interested."

Kells throws an arm around my shoulder and leads me away. "As for you," he says. "You better show up."

"Why?" I say, feeling a little nervous. I know what happens sometimes when Kells gets too close.

"Because I need a chance to win back what I lost, that's why," he says.

"Whoa," I say, backing away, hands in the air. "I don't have that kind of money. I'm still in high school."

Kells chuckles and shakes his head. "I don't mean money," he says. "I've got money."

He turns away and climbs into his car. His thug gets in the passenger seat and they start to roll off, but stop right in front of me and Kim. Kells rolls down the window and adds, "I mean pride."

Then he drives off.

CHAPTER FIFTEEN

"I guess this is goodbye," Kim says as I pull up to her apartment building.

"I'll see you again," I say, hoping it's true. "You can come around and help me work on the Focus some more."

She smiles, but I can tell she's already gone. "Sorry, James," she says. "I'm not sticking around. My debt's cleared, and I don't like the idea of running into Kells again—even by accident."

"Then what will you do?" I say.

She shrugs. "Hit the road," she says. "No

reason to stick around this town anymore."

I look at my hands on the steering wheel. I don't suppose I count as a reason to stick around.

"Aw, James," she says, and she pats my leg. "I like you. But you're young, and you got a lot of years of being young ahead of you. Some girl your age is gonna flip for you."

"Oh, any day now," I say, but I smile, too.

"I promise," she says. Then she kisses me on the cheek and gets out of the car. As she lets herself into her apartment, she doesn't even look back.

* * *

Dad's waiting up for me when I get home. I should be scared to see the light on in the living room, but I'm not. I'm not even surprised.

"Hey," I say as I walk in.

Dad doesn't even get up from the couch. He just looks at me.

"Dad, I didn't have a choice," I say. "I know

you'll probably ground me, and I don't care. You can extend the punishment till I turn eighteen and move out of the house. I would have done it anyway."

I'm about to tell him everything: about picking up Kim on the street a few nights ago, to ending up in Kells's trunk, to the street race tonight. But Dad doesn't even let me start.

"Spare me," he says, raising one hand as he gets up. He's tired—I can see it in his face. "I'm going to assume this has something to do with that girl who was here all day—Kim, wasn't it?"

"Yeah," I say.

He nods and sighs. "I'm going to bed," he says. "You're still grounded, but that's it. Think of this as your one get-out-of-jail-free card. It's not every day you'll find a girl who'll help you get your car to 300 hp, is it?"

He winks and then heads upstairs.

I stand there at the bottom of the steps, still with my car keys in my hand.

No, I think. *It sure isn't.*

THE FORD FOCUS

MODEL HISTORY

The Ford Focus model was launched in Europe in 1998 and in the United States in 2000. The Ford Focus ST was designed as a high-performance version of the original Focus. The ST Focus has recently topped the SVT Focus of previous model years in terms of popularity. The SVT Focus is no longer sold in the United States.

FOCUS ON THE COMPETITION

The Focus has garnered attention worldwide for its success on the racetrack, as well as its superior handling and performance. The Ford Focus first took to the racetrack at the Monte Carlo Rally in 1999. Since its first appearance, the Focus has raced in 173 events, winning 44 of them, placing second in 43, and placing third in 55.

As a testament to car's success, the Focus won the FIA (Fédération Internationale de l'Automobile) World Rally Championship (WRC) manufacturer's title for Ford in 2006 and 2007.

"The Ford Focus RS WRC will be remembered as one of the sport's great rally cars," said Ian Slater, Ford of Europe's Vice-President of Communications and Public Affairs. "It was unveiled at the Paris Motor Show in 1998, exactly at the same time as the Focus road car was launched. The successes of the road and rally models have run in parallel since then."

THE FOCUS AND MODDING

Because the Focus ST is so similar to its racing car equivalent, after-market mods (modifications made after the owner has purchased the car) are fairly common in order to make it the vehicle flashier or sportier. Performance upgrades include cold-air intake system installations, which route more air through the engine to make it more powerful, and exhaust system upgrades. Throttle body installations are also fairly common. These installations control how much air is let in to the engine, increasing the efficiency and power of a vehicle. Another popular mod is to replace the wheels on the vehicle with shinier ones, making it look more like a racing car.

THE FORD FOCUS TODAY

While the Focus ST no longer appears in rally championships, its successor, the Ford Focus

ST-R, debuted at the Frankfurt Automobile Show in 2011. The makeup of the ST-R is not much different than the ST Focus model.

The Ford Focus ST Estate was named Top Gear's "hot hatch of the year" in 2012. The 2013 Focus ST has a six-speed manual transmission and the new Ford Sport Steering System, which promises precise handling thanks to Electric-Power-Assisted Steering (EPAS). With a turbocharged 2.0 liter EcoBoost engine, it can reach 252 horsepower.

JAMES'S FORD FOCUS

ENGINE: turbocharged 250 horsepower, direct fuel injected, front wheel drive 2.0 liter engine; 16 valve inline—4 aluminum block and head; 6-speed manual transmission; installed cold air intake system (this engine definitely likes cold air—the Focus has performed way better since installing it); 0 to 60 acceleration in just over 6 seconds; installed a cat back exhaust system (allows exhaust gases to exit with very little back pressure); new nitrous tank installed (just in time to help me scorch Kells on the track!); performance spark plugs; replaced air filters (these are important because they remove dust and grime from the air flowing into the engine)

DRIVETRAIN: installed SVT short shifter (the SVT vehicle is off the market now, but its parts are still widely available in the used parts market); replaced throttle body (controls the amount of air flowing into the engine—if this is working at its best, the engine will take in more air and exert more power)

SUSPENSION: replaced rubber bushings with polyurethane bushings (enhances handling of the Focus); new front and rear sway bars; tuned spring and damper (for better handling and performance)

BRAKES: power steering and pump line replacement; installed new front and rear brake pads

WHEELS/TIRES: lightweight, but larger, tires; installed rims (for style and performance)

EXTERIOR: tinted windows; painted body with fresh blue coat; converted to power mirrors; replaced fender bulbs; installed rear saleen spoiler (better downforce, traction, and looks sporty!)

INTERIOR: installed foam speaker baffles on front doors (improves sound quality and protects speakers from dirt and moisture); needle calibration on gauge faces

ELECTRONICS: used flash tuner to ramp up the power and performance of the Focus; new speaker system for louder beats; power

programmer (increases gas mileage and horsepower—sweet!)

Check out the rest of the TURBOCHARGED series:

THE
CATCH

FORCED
OUT

HIGH
HEAT

OUT OF
CONTROL

POWER
HITTER

THE
PROSPECT